ALIEN CLONES FROM OUTER SPACE

Two Heads Are Better Than One

H. B. Homzie

Matt Phillips

ALADDIN PAPERBACKS

New York   London   Toronto   Sydney   Singapore

H. B. H.: To Matt, Jonah, and Ari Eisenberg, who make me go *hoopla hoopla* each day, and to Steven Arvanites, my comedy muse.

M. P.: To Mrs. Phillips, the best teacher in the world.

This book is a work of fiction. Any references to historical events, real people, or real locales are used fictitiously. Other names, characters, places, and incidents are the product of the author's imagination, and any resemblance to actual events or locales or persons, living or dead, is entirely coincidental.

First Aladdin Paperbacks edition September 2002

ALADDIN PAPERBACKS
An imprint of Simon & Schuster
Children's Publishing Division
1230 Avenue of the Americas
New York, NY 10020

Designed by Sammy Yuen Jr.
The text of this book was set in CentITC Bk BT 13 pt.

Printed in the United States of America
2 4 6 8 10 9 7 5 3 1

Library of Congress Control Number 2002103394

ISBN 0-689-82342-8

Introduction

My name is Barton Jamison, and I am NOT a freak. Honest. Some people think I'm completely wacky. That's because they've seen me in a tin-foil suit, mowing the living room carpet. But that's not me.

It's my clone, a kid who looks exactly like me. His name is Beta, and he's got a home address in the next galaxy. That's right. He's an alien. And he wants to do all kinds of Earth stuff, even chores.

That means Beta cleans my room while I rule on PlayStation. And he takes out the trash while I go skateboarding. Pretty cool, huh?

Me (Barton) cool

Beta (my clone)

Nancy (my twin sister)

Gamma (Nancy's clone)

But my clone also gets me into BIG trouble.

And guess what? My twin Nancy also has a clone. Which means DOUBLE trouble.

Take last summer, when the whole clone thing started. It was at the playoff game for the town Little League championship. . . .

Chapter 1

BARTON:
Me Sees Me

Our rivals the Rattlers had pulled ahead by three. It was the last inning and the bases were loaded.

With two outs, we needed an awesome hitter to step up to the plate. Someone who could blast the ball right out of the park. Someone who never choked.

Boy, did I feel sorry for the kid up next.

"Now batting for the Mongooses," said the announcer over the loud speaker, "Barton Jamison, number nine."

What? Barton Jamison. That was me! Totally impossible. I was in the bathroom!

I heard chanting. Louder and louder. It sounded like . . . BARTON! BARTON! BARTON!

The game was all on me! I bolted out the bathroom door.

Ahead I could see Coach Holtz pacing back

and forth in front of the dugout. Otto Denzer, my arch enemy, stood on the pitcher's mound, glaring at the batter's box.

"Go get 'em, Barton!" I heard my mom yell. I started to wave at her when I noticed that she was waving at some kid in the batter's box.

Some kid who wasn't me.

I froze behind a tree.

My sister Nancy, who was helping out at the snack hut, whistled at the kid, and my dad pointed his video camera at him. "Hey, buddy," he yelled. "Smile."

I had to be dreaming. The kid looked like a leftover wrapped in foil and ready to be baked.

But for some strange reason, my parents thought he was me. Didn't they know their own son? This was crazy. A walking piece of aluminum was taking over my life.

Whoa, I thought. *There has to be a simple explanation.* I craned my head forward to get a better view. And boy, did I get a view.

The tin foil boy spun around, and I got a good look at his face.

The kid was me!

Chapter 2

BeTA:
Alert! Stink Balls!

Remember: Keep your eye on the ball, Barton," commanded the earthling everyone referred to as Coach.

"Yes, sir!" I said. "But my name is Beta Zeeekwarplatzatot. From the Planet Ungapotch." I ran up to Otto-the-pitcher and stuck my eye on the ball. The earthlings roared with laughter.

Otto yanked the ball away. "Get away, freak. You from another planet or something?"

"So you know the truth," I replied. "I am the alien clone of an earthling."

Coach came up to us and grabbed hold of my special aluminum space suit, and he dragged me toward a boy with a cage-like device over his face. "Listen, Barton. You're in a tinfoil suit, you're acting weird, but you're up! Go to the plate and hit the ball with the bat."

Following the great leader's directions, I raised the bat and looked for a ball to hit. Then I remembered Otto had the ball. I observed him dancing around and singing, "Strike-a-rama, yeah. Strike-a-licious, yeah. I'm taking you out."

"Taking me out?" I said. "I can't wait to go somewhere. I'm excited to see all sorts of earthling sites."

Suddenly the ball whizzed toward me. I swung the bat and hit the white orb. It flew over the stands. The people seated were very happy I had hit the ball to them. They all jumped up to catch it. I was pleased to bring such joy to the earthlings.

"Foul!" a big man behind me screamed. High alert! From watching old TV shows such as *The Three Stooges* and *Scooby-Doo*, I understood Earth ways. Foul means stinky. I plugged my nose unit.

Otto released another stinky ball. I was able to calculate from the angle of release and the rotation of the orb that it was going to fly too close to my face for me to hit it with the wooden stick. Therefore I let it whiz by me.

"Ball one," said the big man this time.

"What are you trying to do, pitcher?" screamed Coach. "Hit my boy? That was a bean-ball if I ever saw one."

Beans? I knew all about beans. A very nutritious, filling, and gassy food. Playing baseball sure made my stomach unit hungry.

I grabbed the ball and popped it into my mouth, which has been specially enhanced to open extra wide. "Mmm, *zaptopkaka!*"—that means wow on my planet! The spectators in the stands roared with appreciation.

Coach charged toward me. "Spit that thing out," he said. I fired the ball out of my mouth.

"Get up to the plate, Barton," Coach commanded. "Hit the ball over the fence."

As I stared into Coach's red face, I finally began to understand. *Hit the ball over the fence?* Let's see, if I simply used my specially enhanced little finger when I swung the bat, the orb would proceed on a linear course over the fence and out into the stratosphere. Why didn't they tell me this was so easy?

I held up my wooden stick, swung, and hit the ball. It sailed into the air, over the fence, straight into the clouds, over the moon, and out of the solar system.

The crowd jumped to their feet, screaming.

Otto threw his glove onto the ground. "NO WAY!" he yelled. "This can't be happening."

"But it is!" I yelled happily.

One by one, the players raced around the field. As they stepped past me, they slapped my back. Oh, *tinglewarp*. I did not mean to make them angry.

Coach waved his hands. "Grand slam! Run the bases, son. Tear 'em up."

Tear up the bases?

6

I picked up the piece of rubber and began to shred it.

Coach raced over and pulled the base away. "No," he yelled. "Go home! HOME! HOME!"

What a strange command. I will make note of it in my *totopapap* journal. How could I ever run the bases back to my home, a million-trillion light-years away? I'd simply have to run into an Earth home.

"*Zaptopkaka!* Bye-bye, earthlings!" I yelled, running off the field and down the street looking for a home.

Chapter 3

BARTON:
Believe It or Not!

As the tinfoil boy zoomed off the field, Coach screamed, "Barton, get back here! You have to run the bases!"

I was still too stunned to move. A boy that looked exactly like me had hit the biggest grand slam of all time.

Hey, wait a moment. What was I doing? All my life I've wished I were homerun hero.

"BARTON!" yelled Coach even louder.

That's when I stepped out from behind the tree. "Over here, Coach," I said, smiling.

"Where's your E.T. outfit?" shouted Otto. "Did you phone it home?"

Coach shook his head. "Get out there, Barton. Run the bases!"

I jogged around the diamond. The grand-slam king waved to his fans.

The people in the stands went crazy, throwing boxes of popcorn into the air. The final score flashed on the scoreboard. Mongooses: 9, Rattlers: 8. We'd won the play-off game! Unbelievable!

We were going to be in the Pine Bluff Little League championship the next day against the Flamingoes. All because of me. . . . At least, another me.

My best friend, Ross Silvers, pointed to my baseball uniform. "That was sure a quick change, Barton." He grinned at me. "You're unbelievable."

"You can say that again," I said out of breath. "Unbelievable."

The next thing I knew, James "the Giraffe" Johnson lifted me up onto his shoulders. James was captain of the Mongooses. "TWO, FOUR, SIX, EIGHT, who do we appreciate? BARTON! BARTON! BARTON!" my teammates cheered.

I never felt so happy in my whole entire life.

"Hey, Barton," said James. "I can't wait to see you do that again during the championship game."

THE CHAMPIONSHIP GAME! The guys were expecting me to hit like . . . a champ.

"Hey, I'll give it my best shot," I said, feeling like a fast ball had hit my gut. "But . . . uh . . . no promises, guys."

"No promises?" asked Ross, as he squirted a bottle of water over my head.

As water dripped off my nose, Otto stomped by and spit out his gum. It landed on my shoe. "I've seen your swing, Barton," he said. "There's no way *you* hit that ball."

All the guys stared at me. For a minute nobody spoke.

Then James elbowed me in the ribs. "Like it was someone else who looked exactly like you who hit a grand slam today."

"Yeah," I said, trying to laugh with the rest of the guys. "That's crazy." And that was the truth. The whole idea that someone else, my double, had hit that ball and then vanished was too weird. Had I been dreaming?

I felt a big hand slap me on the back. It was Coach. And Coach was definitely reality. "One more hit like that and we win it all," said Coach, grinning. "We sure need you, Barton."

"I'll second that," said my dad, zooming up to

me from the stands. "Good job, buddy. Now that's how you play ball!" My mom and sister were right behind him.

"I'm so proud," said Mom, throwing her arms around me. "All that hard work paid off, huh, slugger?"

I nodded weakly.

Nancy tossed me a candy bar. "Way to go, Bart!" My sister stared at my uniform. "Hey, where's that weird space suit?"

"Um, it's in there." I pointed to my duffel bag. Nancy reached over to take a look.

I tried to grab it from my sister. "I wouldn't do that if I were you."

Nancy started to unzip the bag. "Pew. It's like a skunk in there," she said.

She quickly closed the bag.

I breathed a sigh of relief until Dad pointed to my mountain bike locked up by the parking lot. "When you make your way home, we've got a *surprise* for you."

"Surprise?" I asked, my heart pounding. Did they know about the tinfoil boy? "A good surprise?"

"Very," Nancy said, smiling. "My friends are coming over. To the house. And guess what we're making." She poked me in the stomach. "Posters. With your name on them. For the championship game tomorrow."

The championship game. My stomach felt twisted up like a pretzel. What was I going to do about the game tomorrow? Otto was right. That wasn't me who had hit the grand slam. I'm lucky if I get a single.

Now everyone was counting on me. My coach, my teammates, my family, even my sister's friends. This was awful. I had twenty-four hours to turn into a pro slugger.

As my family waved good-bye, I unlocked my bike. Too much was happening. And it was all too weird. Where did that tinfoil kid come from? And where did he go?

And then I got an idea. Maybe I could ask him to hit for me at the big game tomorrow.

But there was one huge problem. The tinfoil kid had raced off the field. He was gone, and I had no idea where to find him!

Chapter 4

BETA:
Feed the Furniture

From my research, I knew that on earth the younger people must do what the older people tell them. If they don't they must go to a dreadful place called Time Out. I did not want to go to a place where time stopped; therefore, I knew I had to obey Coach's orders.

Racing along the streets in my rocket-powered boots, I searched for a suitable home. For a long time, I looked and looked. Until . . .

Zaptopkaka! Inside the window of one of the homes, I detected my sister Gamma with two unknown earthlings. One was tall with long hair the color of a yellow Zorillion meteorite. The other girl was short with hair the color of Ungapotchian mud.

I zoomed into the house. My sister wore strange clothes, and she had painted her fingernails instead of her nose.

"GAMMA! GAMMA! GAMMA!" I yelled. "I am so happy to see you. It has been a trillion-million *gigazaps*."

"Okay," said my sister. "You can start acting normal now."

"Yes, Gamma. I will try to act more Earthlike." I rubbed my sister's elbow three times. Then I grabbed her hair to pull out her antennae.

"GET AWAY!" she yelled.

"You don't wish to tickle antennae, Gamma?"

"Nancy. My name is Nancy. Did the ball hit you on the head? You're acting weird." She looked at me as if I was from another planet.

And then I realized something. This was not my sister. She was Nancy, my sister's Earth clone. How thrilling. I decided to engage the earthling and learn much.

Nancy turned around and showed the females a large, sunken room directly off the hallway. "Sorry about him," she said, pointing at me. "He's acting like such a nerd. We can make the posters in the living room."

The living room? How fascinating—the room

was alive! I looked around eagerly. We had nothing like this on Ungapotch. The floor covering, the pillows, the sitting furniture must be living and breathing creatures!

"Kids!" called up a voice from downstairs. "Dad and I are finding all kinds of good stuff to make banners with down here in the basement. Two old sheets!"

"That's great, Mom!" shouted Nancy.

"Don't forget to make yourself sundaes," called out an adult male's voice.

"Don't worry, Dad," said Nancy, walking into the kitchen. "We won't."

Nancy brought out a couple of bowls of a substance called ice cream and handed them to the female earthlings. "Sierra, Amber," she said, smiling. "Here you go."

Then Nancy went back into the kitchen and returned with an even bigger bowl of ice cream. "For you, Mister Home Run King," she said, setting the dish in front of me.

As Sierra and Amber clapped, I dipped my hand into the cool product. On my fingertip, I watched the ice cream transform into a liquid. It looked exactly like Ungapotchian *goo-goo farkzop*, one of the most powerful substances in the universe. When the girls turned away, I collected some of the melted substance into a vial, as a sample to show our leader, Commander Vortek.

Next I watched as Nancy and her friends poured food products called hot fudge, nuts, whipped cream, and cherries onto their ice cream. Immediately I began to eat the energy source, but then I realized just how rude I was. The furniture and the other creatures in the living room must be hungry too.

I heaped whipped cream onto the end tables and stuffed the cushions on the couch with cherries. "EAT, my little living friends, EAT!" Then I grabbed the jar of hot fudge and dumped it onto the floor.

Fudge splashed onto Amber's dress. "Yuck!" she screamed

Yuck must mean thank you for feeding my dress. "You're welcome," I said.

Nancy threw a cherry-soaked cushion at me. "Doofus! What's your problem? Mom! Dad!" Nancy yelled. "Barton's messing everything up!"

Nancy's mother and father walked into the living room.

"What's going on?" demanded Father.

Nancy pointed to Amber's dress. Then she nodded at the furniture. "Look at what he did."

Mother stared at me. "Did you do this on purpose?"

"Oh, yes!" I exclaimed. "The furniture was very hungry."

Father put his arms on my shoulders. "Buddy, I know you're excited about winning the game, but one more stunt and that's it. No more video games for a week. Got it?" I nodded.

"Girls, let's go up to Nancy's room," said Mother. "Amber, sweetie, you can change into some of Nancy's clothes. I'll throw your dress into the wash."

Water gathered in Amber's eyes. "Do you have Cleanie Detergent?" Mother nodded, and then she and the girls marched upstairs to the bedroom. I remembered that the bedroom is the earthlings' rest chamber.

Shortly thereafter, Mother came back down, carrying the dress. As the Earth parents carried

19

it to the basement, they glared at me. "You better take care of the living room," demanded Mother.

"Barton," said Father. "You heard your mother. Take care of this room! Right now!"

"It will be an honor," I said, looking around me. "And a privilege." But how could I take care of the living room? From my research videos, I knew how human beings took care of living things such as grass and flowers. They chopped, trimmed, and fertilized. I would find a lawn mower to mow the living-room carpet. Afterward I'd fertilize the furniture.

The earthlings would be so pleased.

Chapter 5

BARTON:
I've Lost Myself

Sprinting down the street, I looked everywhere for the tinfoil kid—inside of trash cans, under cars, in backyards, and in open garages. But he had disappeared. And there was nobody around to ask. Finally I saw my neighbor Mrs. Ashcroft. She was watering her petunias.

"Have you seen me?" I asked.

"Yes," said Mrs. Ashcroft, giggling. "You're standing in front of me."

"I mean earlier," I said. "Did you see me earlier?"

Mrs. Ashcroft wound up her green watering hose. "I think you'd know the answer to that question." She started walking to her front door.

I followed her. "You see, I was playing baseball and got hit in the head. And I'm doing an experiment. So did you see me?"

"Yes," said Mrs. Ashcroft opening her screen

door. She looked at me like I had antennae.

"My memory," I said, tapping my head. "It's starting to come back. Just tell me where did I go? What was I doing?"

"Running down the street," said Mrs. Ashcroft. "In shiny disco boots. You went over there." She pointed to a mailbox at the end of the block. The address said 2413. That was my address. The tin-foil boy was in my house!

Chapter **6**

BETA:

Nothing More than Peelings

Nancy stared at the new improved living room. Fertilizer dripped off the curtains. It will make them grow. A river of potting soil oozed through the carpet, which was full of egg shells and apple peels. So many nutrients!

Nancy blinked a few times and pulled on her hair. How happy she must be with my work.

"NO WAY! WHAT DID YOU DO?" she said in an exceptionally loud voice. She must have been very pleased with me!

I smiled. "Exactly what your parents commanded. I took care of the living room. In order to take care of living things you must trim, you must water, you must fertilize!"

"I'm telling Mom and Dad!" said Nancy in her loud voice.

"Don't stop there," I said, clapping my hands

in delight. "Let the entire galaxy know!"

Sierra and Amber marched down the stairs. They froze when they stepped into the living room. Their faces were the color of the red Ungapotchian sky.

"THERE'S GOOP ON MY BACKPACK!" screamed Sierra.

"MY HOMEWORK HAS BEEN SLIMED!" yelled Amber.

"You're welcome," I said, humbly bowing before these Earth girls.

Nancy kicked the goop off the carpet, but a banana peel stuck to her shoe. Sierra and Amber grabbed their belongings and raced out the front door.

My sister's Earth clone was registering displeasure, which was very confusing. "Why are you so upset?" I asked.

"WHY?" said Nancy. "You ruined everything!" She whirled around. "Go flush yourself down the toilet!"

"I will do as you command." Immediately, I walked to the bathroom.

Chapter 7

BARTON:
Flush Away!

NANCY!" I cried, walking into the house. "MOM, DAD!"

"Barton!" yelled Nancy. "You better get back here and help me clean up this mess."

"I was just here?" I asked hopefully, following her voice into the living room.

"Yeah," said Nancy. "Like five seconds ago."

"You didn't see where I went, did—oh, no! What happened?" I couldn't believe what I saw. Our living room looked like a garbage dump!

"Like you don't know." Nancy stood in the middle of the room. She looked madder than I've ever seen her.

"Did I do this?" I asked. "Oh, wow. This is crazy. . . . I can't believe it. It's . . . big stuff. I think I'm in—"

"BIG TROUBLE!" yelled Mom, marching into the living room.

Dad stomped in right behind her. "No video games or TV for a week."

Mom stared at Dad like he was crazy. "A week? How about a month? Three months. The whole year!" She stared at the trash filled carpet. Then her eyes went up to the muddy curtains. "I just special ordered those. Barton, what were you thinking? What?!"

I took a step backwards. "Something came over me. It was like I was someone else."

"You had better explain that, mister," said Dad.

"And that," said Mom, pointing to the lawn mower parked in front of the fireplace.

"A . . . uh . . . science project?" I said. "For extra credit. I wanted to study the lawn mower. In the living room. That's when it went berserk. And mowed the carpet. All by itself."

"Barton, stop while you're behind," said Mom. "Tell us the truth." She counted on her fingers. "Why did you throw hot fudge onto Amber, spray my furniture with whipped cream and cherries, mow the living carpet, and fertilize the furniture? I'm very curious. We all are."

Mom had her hands on her hips, Nancy clenched her teeth, and Dad's face was scary white. They stared at me, waiting for an answer.

My palms got all sweaty. I swallowed hard. "Okay, here's the truth. It wasn't me. But a kid dressed in an aluminum suit who happens to look exactly like me. I wasn't even here. I was out searching for myself. Well, not myself. But the other me."

Mom put her fingers into her hair. She opened her eyes really wide and opened her mouth so you could see her back cavities. It was her most scary look. "The one thing I cannot tolerate is a liar," she said. "The one thing! And this room is a wreck. If I stand here one more second I'm going to be sick."

Moaning, Mom ran upstairs and Dad followed her. But then he turned around and said in a calm but firm voice, "You better clean up this mess, Barton."

"But . . . but . . . it wasn't me," I babbled. "Honest."

After the door to my parent's bedroom slammed shut, Nancy shook her head. "Uh huh," said Nancy. "A kid dressed in tinfoil who just happens to look exactly like you did this? That's so dumb."

"But it's true. I have to find him. Really, really fast. He's got to hit for me tomorrow at the championship game. I didn't hit the grand slam today. . . . He did."

Nancy stared at me. "What are you talking about?"

"Look, I know it's beyond weird," I said. "But you've got to believe me."

I started picking up eggshells off the floor when I thought of something.

If that tinfoil kid just left a few minutes ago, he couldn't have gone far. I had to find him and get some answers.

I looked at my sister. "Where did I go exactly? If I was just here."

Nancy shrugged her shoulders.

That's when we heard a flush.

"I think you're trying to flush yourself down the toilet," she said.

BARTON:
My Face to My Face

I raced to the bathroom and opened the door.

The aluminum kid had his head in the toilet. He kept scooping and flushing. Scooping and flushing.

"Just who are you and why do you look exactly like me?" I demanded.

The boy pulled his head up and grinned. "It's quite simple," he said. Soggy toilet paper covered his face. "I am your alien clone from outer space."

"My alien clone from outer space," I said. "Oh, I get it. The whole thing makes sense to me now. MY CLONE FROM OUTER SPACE? Are you crazy? My alien clone from outer space? I've seen *Star Wars* ten times. No way you're an alien."

"I'm Beta Zeeekwarplatzatot," he said, "from

the planet Ungapotch, the nearest planet to the Milky Way in the Zorillion Galaxy. I've traveled across time and space in order to fulfill my mission to learn about Earth life."

"If you're an alien," I pointed out, "how come you don't look like one, huh?"

That's when antennae popped out of Beta's head.

"Nancy!" I screamed "GET OVER HERE!" My sister raced down to the bathroom.

She stared at me and then at the other me. "Barton?" she gasped. "Barton? What's going on? There are two of you! Barton! This isn't funny." She pointed to Beta. "He's wiggling antenna eyeballs at me!"

"I am your brother's alien clone," said Beta. "Your clone from outer space should arrive shortly."

"*MY* CLONE!" exclaimed Nancy. "WHAT?"

Beta nodded. "Biologically, she's exactly like you," he explained. "With a few enhancements."

Nancy shook her head in amazement. "How did they clone us?"

"Your DNA was scraped off your baloney

sandwiches by scouts from our planet," said Beta. "Our scientists chose you because they felt you perfectly represented average, ordinary Earth children. So you were duplicated for friendly missions to learn about earth life."

"Oh, no way," said Nancy. "No way. No way."

"Yes way!" Beta nodded his antennas. "Past missions have been unsuccessful at learning about Earth life. When our scientists came to collect data, human beings screamed, 'UFO!' They seemed to exhibit extreme fear of Ungapotchians in our normal form. We are the ugliest species in the Milky Way, you know. So our top officials decided to duplicate Earth children so we would fit right in as we collected information about life on your planet."

"This is so neat! I bet you guys have lots of cool stuff," I said, thinking about alien gadgets like zappers and ray blasters. "But why us?" I asked. "Why a couple of kids?"

"Because," Beta explained, "from the research tapes we observed, we learned that it is the young people who have the most new experiences. Older earthlings—grown-ups, I believe

34

you call them—spend most of their time drinking a fluid called coffee and talking about the weather. Therefore, we decided that creating younger clones would give us the greatest opportunity to learn the most about life on Earth. One family we studied in particular was the Bradys. Do you know them? They seem to come in a bunch."

Before I could explain to Beta the difference between TV and real life, he handed me a clear tube filled with some kind of white liquid with brown swirls. "I have collected some cool stuff. Back on Ungaptoch we call it *goo-goo farkzop*. We spread it on ourselves and feel the power."

"Thanks, Beta. Wow." I grabbed the vial and stuck it in my pocket. "What I'm really wondering is if you could hit for me tomorrow in the championship game."

Beta looked at a miniature computer strapped to his wrist. "No time to talk," he said. "My sister Gamma sent me a signal. She's landing in ten *gigazaps*."

Nancy threw her arms around me. "My clone is coming!"

"Earthlings," announced Beta, firing up his rocket-powered boots, "I'm off to the landing site. Until Gamma touches down, I will wait in the large receptacle filled with energy supplies next to the baseball field where I enjoyed playing hit the white orb with a stick."

He waved his antennae. "Follow me." Beta zipped his aluminum suit, grabbed his bubble-shaped helmet and then zoomed out the door in rocket-powered boots. The force from his take-off knocked over the lamps in the living room.

I looked at Nancy. "Do you think he'll hit for me tomorrow?"

"I don't know," said Nancy, pulling me by the hand. "But how many times do you get to see your clone from outer space land? Grab your bike. Let's go!"

Chapter 9

BETA:
One Gigazap!

Rocketing down the street, I approached the landing site. In less than one *gigazap* Gamma would touch down. I turned into the park.

But I could not continue my journey. A large earthling stood in the middle of the road, waving his fist. "You're not going to play in the big game tomorrow after I get through with you." It was Otto-the-pitcher.

"Sorry, I don't have time for communication with you, my friend. My sister, Gamma, who has been traveling for a million-billion-trillion light-years will be landing her space ship in the large receptacle near where you threw the white orb at me." I looked at my chronometer. "In one half a *gigazap*."

"You've lost your brain!" said Otto.

"No," I said, tapping my head. "It's stored right

here. I don't have time to take it out and show you. I must go now to meet my sister."

As I zoomed away, Otto was blown to the ground. I could heard him screaming at me, "Barton, you're dead meat!" Did Otto eat children?

Chapter 10

BARTON:
Alien pepperoni pizza

Nancy and I pedaled our bikes after Beta. But in his rocket-powered boots he had flown way ahead of us.

Entering the park, we raced toward the Dumpster near the baseball field. We figured that's where he was headed though we weren't a hundred percent sure. Unfortunately, we soon discovered Otto *was* there.

He knocked me off my bike and pushed me hard up against the fence. "BARTON!" he screamed. "YOU MESSED UP MY SHIRT!"

"That wasn't me," I sputtered. "That was my—"

"Let him go!" shouted Nancy, pulling on me.

"Uh, sorry about that, Otto," I said stepping away from him. "But I had nothing to do with it. Really."

"Yeah right, dork," snarled Otto. "You just told

me your sister was about to land her spaceship." He stared at Nancy. "Love your spaceship, Nancy," he said, kicking the tires of her bike. Then he lunged for me. "Tell me more, space boy."

As I was backing away from Otto, I glanced up. And I couldn't believe what I saw. A long, curved spaceship hovered over the Dumpster. "Look!" I shouted.

Otto and Nancy both stared at the space ship. Well, not a ship exactly. More like a space cigar. It was lit at one end and blew stinky smoke. Here I was, Barton Jamison, actually witnessing a real UFO. The thing that surprised me the most was how simple looking it was. There were no doors or windows. As the ship started to hum, I held my breath.

"What's going on?" shouted Otto. "I know you're up to something, Barton."

The ship landed in the Dumpster, which started shaking. Puffs of green smoke shot out. Chicken bones, soda cans, candy wrappers, notebooks, gum, garlic mashed potatoes, tomatoes, and sour milk spewed out of the top like a volcano.

"Barton, you can't fool me!" yelled Otto. "That's not a real UFO." Just then a half-eaten pepperoni pizza blindsided him. "Oww! What was that?" Cheese stuck to his eyelids and nose. "Help!" he screamed, backing away. "I'm being attacked by an alien pepperoni pizza!"

He desperately tried to pull the cheese off his face.

A Pop-Tart smacked Nancy in the head and a chicken wing hit me on the nose.

Suddenly all the green smoke stopped pouring out of the ship and the lights dimmed.

A girl who looked exactly like my sister jumped out of a little hatch in the middle of the ship. She wore a tinfoil suit just like Beta's, only hers had a purple tint to it. "What's down?" she asked. "I mean, what's up? The name is Gamma."

Nancy stared at Gamma. And Gamma stared at Nancy. Same eyes, same ears, same nose, same mouth.

"You look just like me!" shouted Nancy. "WOW!"

"Jubilation. Glee. Glee. My earth clone!" Gamma jumped up and down and stood on her tongue.

Then Beta rose up out of the Dumpster.

Otto stared at Beta, then looked back at me, checking and rechecking what he saw. He pointed and babbled, "There's one . . . two Nancy's and one . . . two Bartons. One. Two. Two of you! NO!"

Otto's head continued to ping-pong back and forth. "The piece of tinfoil hit the homerun. An . . . alien . . . freaky . . . garbage . . . alien . . . INFESTATION!"

Otto staggered out of the park, screaming, with cheese still dangling off his chin.

Chapter 11

BETA:

Attic Fans

As Otto raced away, Gamma swung me around by my antennae. "Jubilation, sister!" I shouted. "Glee! Glee!"

Gamma grinned and looked at herself in my reflective fleet suit. "Do you think my antennae look shiny?"

I nodded. "On Earth, however, we must keep them retracted. I have learned much about Earth ways from"—I grinned—"our Earth clones, Barton and Nancy."

"I am so honored to meet and greet you," Gamma said. "Now we must proceed with our information harvest."

I smiled at Barton. "If you need to reach us, use this," I said, handing Barton the *snogelplat.* "Press this purple button. In an emergency we can beam ourselves to your exact location."

Barton looked as if he had never seen a *snogelplat* before. "Cool," he said, staring at the buttons. "A clone phone."

"But never touch the green button," warned Gamma. "It's the converter. You turn green. Temporarily, of course. We use it to camouflage ourselves during emergencies."

We waved our antennae good-bye and then retracted them.

"Hey, wait a minute," said Nancy. "Where are you going to live?"

"Fuel receptacle," said Gamma, smiling. "We have found your energy supplies quite tasty." She pointed to a pile of chicken bones in the trash.

"Eew, gross," said Nancy. "That's garbage. You guys can't eat that. You need to eat real food. And stay someplace nice, like a house."

"You can stay in the attic above our garage," said Barton.

"No way!" said Nancy. "Are you crazy? Did you see what Beta *did* to the house? And what about Otto? He knows everything."

"C'mon, Nance," I begged. "It's no big deal. Otto won't know a thing. The clones can't cause any damage if they stay in the attic. There's nothing for them to mess up in there."

She grabbed the *snogelplat* away from Barton. "Well, if they're going to live in the garage, I'm going to take the clone phone."

"*Zaptopkaka!*" said Gamma. "We will live with our Earth clones!"

I felt overwhelmed with gratitude. What luxury! We would live in an attic with real cobwebs and mice. "What else can we do to help you?" I asked, rising in the air in my rocket-powered boots.

Barton smiled. "One more thing: Can you hit another home run for me tomorrow?"

"No," Nancy said, shaking her head. "What if Otto's at the game?"

Barton folded his arms. "Don't worry. Otto isn't playing."

"How disappointing," I said. "Nevertheless, I'm overjoyed to participate in such an important endeavor. Another game of 'hit the orb with the stick.' *Hoopla. Hoopla.*"

"Listen," Barton said, putting his arm around my shoulder. "You seem like a real smart guy. Here's a few things you need to learn. It's not 'hit the orb with the stick.' It's called baseball. The stick's a bat. The orb's a ball. Got it?"

I popped out my antennae and nodded them.

"So here's what we're going to do," said Barton. "Tomorrow at the game, I'm going to sit on the bench with my teammates." He grabbed the *snogelplat* back from Nancy. "Right before I'm up to bat, I'll run to the bathroom and call you," he said, tapping the purple button. "We'll switch places. Nobody will see us. It's that simple."

Gamma twirled around. "May we both attend

46

the game? I want to chronicle this baseball endeavor. It would be more than, as you say, awesome. It would be lofty!"

Barton shut his eyes and thought hard. He tapped his chin, which must be where his brain resides. "I think it'd be better if you were at the game, but you'll have to wear disguises."

"Disguises!" said Nancy, clapping her hands. "Barton, that's brilliant. The clones can work in the snack hut. I promised to help out, but I really want to sit with Amber and Sierra."

The snack hut! I knew all about Earth snacks from commercials. What an honor to work closely with carbonated beverages and salty treats. I couldn't wait to document this rare opportunity and report it to Zortek, our commander.

Our Earth clones took us back to their house and up to the attic. Nancy opened up a dark, square box.

"Here," she said, handing us hairy creatures with no mouth, eyes, feet, or hands. "Wigs for your disguises."

Gamma cradled the dear little wig and began

stroking it. "He reminds me of my pet *woozie* back on Ungapotch," she said.

Barton threw up his arms. "No, no. It's a wig. It's not alive."

Nancy yanked my wig and placed it on my head. "It's so nobody will recognize you." And then she pulled out dark goggles. "Sunglasses. Nobody will suspect a thing."

"And whatever you do don't tell anyone you're alien clones," Barton warned. "Try to act normal."

"Normal?" I asked. "What is normal?"

Chapter **12**

BARTON:
Mean and Green!

Every person in Pine Bluff showed up to see me hit a grand slam at the championship game against the Flamingoes—toddlers with binkies, senior citizens, even teachers.

The Mongooses fans started chanting, "Barton! Barton! Barton!"

Nancy, Amber, and Sierra held up their posters. My parents waved a banner: WE ARE THE PROUD PARENTS OF BARTON THE GRAND-SLAM KING!

In the dugout all the guys crowded around me. "So Barton, right after you swing, you shout *zaptopkaka*, right?" asked James.

"Uh, yeah," I said. "*Zaptopkeke.*"

"*Kaka*," corrected Ross.

"Sometimes I vary it," I said.

"You're so cool, Barton," said Ross. "Bet pro scouts will be out there."

Scouts. Wow. But I decided to act modest. "Scouts, shmouts. Those guys drive me nuts. I've decided to wait a while before going pro. You know, finish my education, get to the fifth grade. My agent is fielding offers after recess."

As Ross walked up to the batter's box, I reassuringly patted the clone phone. I was fourth in the lineup. Time to call my clone. I pointed to the bathroom. "Be right back," I said. "Hope you brought cameras. History in the making."

I ran to the bathroom and took out the phone.

Suddenly I saw Otto standing by the sink. Before I could do anything, he grabbed the phone from me.

"Hey, that's mine!" I yelped.

"Yeah, so?" He put his finger over the giant green button.

"NO!" I yelled. "DON'T PUSH THAT BUTTON!"

"And who's going to stop me," said Otto. "Here's my finger," sang Otto. "It's going to press. Look at me. This button is so easy to press. Press-a-rama! Press-a-licous!"

He gave an evil laugh and pushed the button. That's when he began to glow. And not just a

51

regular glow. His whole face turned swamp green.

I pointed at him. "Otto, you're green."

"I'm not green," he said about to push the button again.

That's when he looked at his hand. "I'M GREEN!" he screamed. "I've been turned into KERMIT THE FROG!"

Then he took off. And with the clone phone. I raced after him but couldn't see him anywhere. But Coach saw me.

"Barton," called out Coach. "You're on deck."

"I've lost something!" I shouted. "And it's *really, really* important."

"Look for it later," said Coach. He walked over and guided me back to the dugout. "Grab a helmet and a bat and get on deck."

Ross looked at me concerned. "Barton? You okay?"

"Ah . . . no," I said, an idea forming. "I've got this really bad stomachache. Don't . . . think I . . . oh, ow . . . can hit." I grabbed my stomach. "It's terrible."

"Okay, Barton," said Coach. "Calm down. Take

a break." I took off my batting helmet and handed James the bat. Now I just had to switch with Beta. That should be easy since he was in the snack hut. I started to jog over there.

But a vice grip pulled me back. "Nobody off the bench," said Coach. "It's bad luck." He stared at me. "If you can't play, clap for your team."

Ross sat next to me on the bench and shook his head. "C'mon and play. A grand slammer like you wouldn't let his team down."

"Sorry." I sighed. My reputation was quickly going down the drain.

I looked over at the snack hut. At least those clones had their disguises on. They couldn't be getting into too much trouble.

CHAPTER 13

BeTA:
Candy Pants

Gamma and I each held the boy by his hand and shook him back and forth. When he looked like he had enough, we set him back on the ground.

The child ran away screaming. "I'm telling my mommy!"

I scratched my nose unit. "Very odd. The little boy said he wanted a shake, so we shook him. These earthlings are very complicated."

There were so many snack products to take care of and experience. I opened a door called freezer section. "More *goo-goo farkzop*, known as ice cream on Earth. And so cold. *Brr.* Must be warmed up. This should work." I stuck the carton of ice cream into the microwave oven. And another and another until all of the frozen treats were hot and in a liquid state. This would make them much easier to consume.

Next I noticed a sealed jar of popcorn kernels. "Nancy said we need to produce plenty of popcorn." I stared at the small little pieces.

"Those are seeds," said Gamma. "We must plant them so they grow." We dug a hole in the bottom of the floor of the snack hut, which was most difficult, as it was metal. Using our enhanced little fingers to cut through the steel, my sister and I placed the popcorn seeds into the hole and covered them with dirt.

"Now we must water the popcorn plants," said Gamma.

"Here is liquid," I said, pointing to something marked cola. I poured the fizzy beverage into the hole.

"I wonder why my earthling did not contact me on the *snogelplat*. He must not want me to hit the white orb with a stick for him." I sighed. "Oh, well. Let us make the cotton candy."

"Cotton," said Gamma, "is a natural fiber that earthlings use to make clothes and bedding products."

I whirled around. "How strange. Earthlings eat

clothing. But I will proceed with the mission." I ripped off the sleeves of my shirt and Gamma ripped off the bottom of her pants. We stuffed them into the cotton-candy machine and added lots of sugar. The smell of the candy pants and shirt was most delightful.

It attracted a long line of customers. However, for some strange reason they passed-up the liquid ice cream and candy clothing. And nobody wanted to purchase a popcorn plant. We sold mostly chocolate and something called licorice, which looked like Ungapotchian hair.

Then Nancy came to check on us. As she approached, Nancy's eyes grew big and round. She must be so pleased. "There's stuff everywhere!" She stood on tiptoes and peaked in. "What happened? Was there an earthquake?"

I shook my head. "No, we've been busy creating cotton candy and other earthling treats. I have had much time to do so, as Barton has not called me on the *snogelplat*."

Just then Mother approached. Nancy hissed, "Don't take off your disguises. Don't talk!"

Mother stared at Gamma and me. "You look

really familiar. Do I know your mother and father?"

Nancy shook her head. "Not possible. They're new in town."

Mother gave a big chuckle and then nodded at me. "I swear I've seen you somewhere before."

"Negative. I'm supposed to be here in the snack hut," I said. "May I offer you something? I know just the thing." Mother would love one of those cartons of hot bubbling ice cream.

Chapter 14

BARTON:
Swap Shop

I couldn't believe that Otto had taken the clone phone. At least he turned green. But where did that leave me? Stuck in the dugout, that's where, listening to my friends beg me to play.

Finally, during the last inning Coach let me off the bench. I raced to the snack hut. We were down by one run. There was still time for Beta to switch places with me and save the day. Opening the side door, I raced into the snack hut.

I popped up by the counter and found myself face to face with my mother and Nancy. Gamma stood in the middle of the snack hut pouring cotton-candy syrup on her shirt. My heart started to pound wildly.

My mother stared at me. And I stared back at her. For a moment neither one of us spoke. Nancy looked very pale.

"Barton, what are you doing here?" asked Mom. "Why aren't you in the dugout?"

"Coach said I could get a drink," I said. "Um, one sec. I need to check on something." Very carefully, I pulled Gamma with me to the back of the hut.

"Where's Beta?" I asked her.

She pointed to the front of the snack hut. "He went that way," she said. "He is serving a most honored customer. Your mother."

Chapter 15

BETA:

The Drink is on Me

I held on the carton of warmed ice cream. "Here. That will be one dollar." It slouched onto the counter.

"No thanks," said Mother. "I wanted a candy bar."

Suddenly Barton appeared next to me in the hut. I felt him pulling on my belt.

"Barton, get back to the game," said Mother. "Let's go. Grab a soda. It's on me."

Drink is on her? That would make her wet and fizzy. That can't be.

I grabbed a candy bar and filled up a cup with fizzy soda.

Handing the candy bar to Mother, I said, "You will be most pleased." I dumped the soda on my head instead. "The drink is on me!"

Fizzy liquid dripped off my nose. My hair was plastered against my head.

60

Mother stared at me and shook her finger. "I want to speak to your parents. Who raised you?" She sounded truly interested in learning everything about me. I felt so happy.

"I'm from another planet and was raised by shiny robots," I explained. "And . . ."

Barton put his arm around me. "And he's not feeling that well. He was hit on the head. And is feeling dizzy. And confused. Let me take him to the back. To lie down. His mother will pick up him later. She's . . . uh . . . working."

As Barton led me to the back of the hut, he whispered, "Otto took the

clone phone. I couldn't call you to switch places."

"Not for long," I said, taking out my super magno reverter. I squeezed the tiny device, which was no bigger than a pea. It went *blippety aka aka*, and the clone phone flew back into my Earth clone's hands.

"Cool," said Barton, staring at the phone. "Now it's time to switch."

As quickly as possible, we swapped clothes. Happily I placed the baseball cap on my head, and Barton put on my wig and dark spectacles. I stuffed a swatch of candy cotton into my pockets.

My earth clone smiled at me. "Go on out there," he said. "Act like me and hit a homer!"

I zoomed out of the hut, clapping my hands. "Hoopla. Hoopla. I will once again experience this earthling endeavor." This was truly thrilling. As I made way to the field, I noticed Otto-the-pitcher walking the other way. He was slightly green in color. What an improvement. I took out my cotton candy and began to snack.

Otto stared at me and pointed. "Hey, only one person is that goofy. . . . That's . . . I know who you are. . . . You're . . . AN ALIEN CLONE!"

Chapter 16

BARTON:
I'm Only Human

From the back of the snack hut, I watched Beta approach the batter's box. Soon he'd be hitting another homer.

But suddenly I saw Otto charge over to the announcer's box. He grabbed the mike. "I've got an announcement," he yelled. "That is an alien clone, and I'm going to prove it."

I watched as Otto ran towards the batter's box. He grabbed Beta's head and started to yank. He was going to pull out Beta's antennae. They would spring out any second. I had to do something!

Opening the back of the snack hut, I peered out. Everybody's eyes were on the fight on the field. The whole baseball game had turned into one big mess. The umpire was rolling around in the dirt. The two coaches were running around in circles. All the players from the dugouts were on the field. Kids were throwing popcorn and licorice laces. It was crazy.

I pulled out the clone phone and pushed.

I heard a crack and a zap, and Beta was materializing in front of me. "You stay here, Beta. I'm going to hit. We've got to keep you a secret and keep your mission safe."

After Beta put the disguise back on, I walked out of the snack hut and began jumping up and down and waving my arms. "Yoo-hoo, Otto. I'm over here!"

Everyone stopped fighting. All eyes were on me.

Otto pointed at me. "That's not Barton. I know he looks like Barton, but it's a trick. This guy's an ALIEN! I know 'cause I just had his space communicator, only he zapped it away from me. He's going take over the whole planet! And he's got a space ship. In the Dumpster. I saw him park it in there. With my own eyes. And he's not just a regular kind of alien. He's Barton's space clone. And he's going to hit for Barton!"

Coach ran up to Otto and started to drag him away.

But Otto broke free. He pushed through like the Incredible Hulk. "I can prove he's an alien," screamed Otto. "He's got antennae!"

"Boo!" screamed the crowd. "BOO!"

"They're retractable!" screamed Otto. "See!" He grabbed onto my head and started digging his fingernails into my scalp like he was going to pull out my brains. "There should be two little holes. I KNOW THERE ARE HOLES IN HIS HEAD!"

Coach and the umpire tried to pull Otto off of me. But they couldn't. His hands were like suction cups on my head.

"I'm a human being. I'm me—Barton," I whispered furiously, and pushed him away.

Otto fell backwards and ran off the field. "I'll prove it!" he screamed.

Otto might be gone, but my life was still doomed. I looked at the scoreboard. The Flamingoes were ahead by one run, the bases were loaded, and I was up to bat.

Now they weren't going to see a baseball hero. They were going to see a baseball zero.

Chapter 17

BeTA:

A Brain Slurpie

I noticed that Otto was wandering through the crowd looking for clones. He waddled up to an elderly earthling with a hearing aid.

"Are you a clone?" he asked.

"What?" asked the elderly earthling.

"I SAID, ARE YOU A CLONE?"

"Are you a phone?" asked the earthling.

"Forget it." Otto turned around, singing. "I'm gonna find a clone. Clone-a-rama. Clone-a-licious!" Gamma and I sprinted behind the bleachers, but Otto spotted us. "Stupid sunglasses. And wigs. Let me have a look." He pulled off our hairpieces. Then he knocked off my spectacles.

Otto turned to me. His eyes grew wide. "You two . . . you're the CLONES!"

"You're right," said Gamma, whispering.

"We are clones." She turned to me. "Let's suck out his memory cells."

"Affirmative," I said. "Otto is becoming quite a *koko*." That's jerk in Ungapotchian.

We bent over Otto's head, pulled out our special brain straws, and, in hyperwarp speed, slurped up part of his memory.

Otto shook and shimmied, turned greener, and then blew his lips. Then he grew quiet and pointed above his head. "What a beautiful sky."

The crowd was quite enthusiastic, screaming, "Barton! Barton! Barton!"

The pitcher threw the ball so high that it almost hit Barton's head. "Ball two! Count two and oh!" yelled the umpire.

Nancy sniffled. "It's too late. There's no way you can switch places with him now."

Barton hit a ball that headed foul. I plugged my nose.

As Coach Holtz shook his head, Barton turned redder than Martian soil. His forehead wrinkled; his chin quivered. I detected water collecting near his eyeballs. High alert! High alert! My

Earth clone was experiencing sadness.

"I must help Barton out." I powered my rocket boots in anticipation.

Nancy grabbed me. "NO!" she screamed. "You can't go onto that field!" She held me back. "But don't worry. Look, it's okay. Barton's putting on that *goo-goo farkzop*." We watched as Barton slathered the liquid onto his arms. "Now he's got alien super powers," said Nancy, smiling.

"Alien super powers?" asked Gamma. "I do not think so."

I nodded. "Barton asked for a cool substance so I gave him what you on Earth call melted ice cream."

Chapter 18

BARTON:
Hero or Zero?

I slathered the alien power lotion all over my hands and arms. It felt sticky and smelled like vanilla ice cream. As I spread it around, I could already feel the power.

Why hadn't I thought about the *goo-goo farkzop* before? Now I'd have alien abilities. And *wham!* I'd smack that ball right out of the park.

Suddenly, the umpire marched up to me. "And what's that?" he demanded staring at my *goo-goo farkzop.*

"It's, uh, bug repellant," I said.

"Hey, I could use some of that." He took some of the goo and sniffed it. "Smells good. Kind of sweet."

Then coach asked for some. And then Ross, James the Giraffe, and all of the kids on my team.

70

The whole team was soon covered with alien *goo-goo farkzop*. Who knew what we could do? Probably break all the bats in two with our bare hands. Hit the ball all the way to Canada.

The ball came spinning towards me. I watched in amazement as I could see the red stitching.

I hit and . . .

The ball sailed out over the field.

"A double for number nine, Barton Jamison!" yelled the announcer. I watched in amazement as two of our guys made it home. Not a home run, but I'd take it. The *goo-goo farkzop* had worked. I won the game!

I was about to get lifted up when James yelled, "Your bug repellant stinks!" Flies and bees buzzed all around my bat.

I laughed weakly.

"Look at all of them," said James, pointing to the swarm of insects, now on my hands—everyone's hands, in fact.

"What is this stuff?" asked Ross, desperately shooing yellow jackets off his arms.

Otto stuck out his hand. "Good job, Barton," he said. "So glad we're buddies."

I couldn't believe it. This was the impossible. Wow, those clones must have vacuumed Otto's brain or something.

I searched the stands. Sure enough, there were the clones. Beta waved his elbow at me and then put his thumb into the air. I gave him a thumbs-up back, then threw in an elbow wave, too. Beta was awesome! There was no doubt about it! I loved that extraterrestrial like family. Come to think of it, in a weird way he sort of was.

All the guys streamed out of the dugout and hoisted me onto their shoulders. "BARTON!" they screamed. "BARTON!" All the fans in the stands were clapping and screaming.

"That's MY boy!" yelled Mom.

"SLUGGER OF THE YEAR!" shouted Dad, who was really grinning.

I saw Beta and Gamma raced out of the stands and onto the field to join the celebration. Luckily they still had disguises on. The clones were with Nancy, Amber, and Sierra. As I joined them, I said to Beta, "Thanks for the alien *goo-goo farkzop*."

"Alien *goo-goo farkzop?*" he said. "Negative. It

73

was from Earth. You asked for something cool so I gave you some melted ice cream I had collected as a sample."

"You mean it was me who hit the double?" I gasped. "Not some special alien goo?"

Beta nodded. Wow, I thought. Maybe I could hit after all.

A photographer from the Pine Bluff Herald took a picture of the big celebration with me, Barton Jamison, being hoisted into the air.

The hero and not the zero. Pretty cool, huh? And that's all because I have a clone of my own. Someone with awesome abilities who comes from an advanced civilization. Someone who really wants to help me out and experience everything about Earth life—everything.

Let's see. On Monday I have to mow the lawn; on Tuesday I have a science quiz; and on Thursday I have to clean out the litter box. The possibilities are endless. . . .